for Precious Little Girls Everywhere

A Little Bit of Faith

By Cindy Kenney
Illustrated by the Precious Moments Creative Studio

Library of Congress Control Number 2008926345
Kenney, Cindy, A Little Bit Of Faith/Cindy Kenney for Precious Moments, Inc.
SUMMARY: Katie Bennett moves to a new town in the middle of a school year
and finds a way to earn friendship through the creation of the Precious Girls Club.

ISBN # 978-0-9817159-1-9

Manufactured in China

Table of Contents

CHAPTER ONE
Squished!

Do you ever wonder why you were born in Topeka, Kansas—Omaha, Nebraska—Flagstaff, Arizona—or wherever it is that you came from? Or maybe you wonder why you were born on the very day—at the exact hour, minute and second that you came into the world.

I sure have.

In fact, I wonder why God gave me the parents He did—and the job my Daddy has—and why the winters here are so cold and windy! To be honest, I wonder about a whole bunch of things— especially since we moved to a little town called Shine, Wisconsin, this past summer.

I wonder about that stuff all the time . . . or what it would be like if things were different. But they aren't.

I was super happy to hear that we were going to live in the same town as my favorite aunt—Aunt Ella. She's my Mom's sister and the nicest, kindest, most creative person and the best cook I've ever met. She always says that she takes "quite a shinin' " to me, too.

The truth is that my whole life has been topsy-turvy ever since we moved to Shine. It's not just my house and neighborhood that changed. I got a brand-new school with new teachers that do things new ways. And the kids in Shine—well, we didn't take a "shinin' " to each other one little bit. Do you know how terrible that can be for a little girl?

I was sitting in my new living room, dreading another day at my new school, when my sister came into the room, plopped down in a chair and started to read.

"Anna!" I shrieked. "You SQUISHED her!"

Anna jumped up and looked in the chair. She probably thought I'd put a lizard or toad there.

I do that sometimes. God says that we should share what we have with others, but for some reason I can get in the worst trouble when I do.

"Katie Marie Bennett, what in the world are you talking about?" Anna asked. "There's nothing in this chair."

"Faith was sitting there," I insisted, "until you SQUISHED her! She's not as big as you and I are, you know! We were having a conservation about that new school I have to go to."

"Conver-SA-tion," corrected Anna as she sat back down to read.

"Yep, one of those . . . until you squished her so flat that I can't even see her now!"

Anna put her book down with a big huff and a puff and rolled her eyes at me. Mom says that it's not polite to get all puffed up like that, but Anna does it all the time.

"Faith is not a *real* angel, Katie," said Anna. "She is a pretty little angel in a musical snow globe that Daddy gave you as a gift. When are you going to stop being such a baby and quit pretending she's real?"

"Faith *is* my guardian angel and she *is* real, Anna. You're just jealous that the angel Daddy gave you *isn't*!"

"Ruff! Ruff!" barked Patches. I don't think he likes it when people fight.

"C'mon, Patches," I said, running up the stairs so Anna couldn't see me cry. Patches followed right behind. I'm not a baby—honest I'm not. I just wish Anna believed that Faith *is* a real, live angel.

I curled up on my bed with Patches, thinking back to when Daddy gave us our angel snow globes. We were both sad about leaving our friends back in Illinois, and he wanted to cheer us up. I took one look at Faith dancing around in her snowy white globe and thought she was the most beautiful thing I'd ever seen!

Later that night, when I was packing, I wound

up the music box on the snow globe. There was a big WHOOSH and Faith flew right out of that glittery snow and sat down next to me! I thought I was dreaming—and that made Faith giggle. I couldn't stop staring at her, and Faith told me that it wasn't very polite. But I couldn't help it! It's not every day a kid gets to see an angel fly out of a snow globe!

She started talking and we got along just as good as milk and cookies. She listens to me when I talk, and somehow she always knows the right thing to say to make me feel better. Before long I said, "Faith, you're the best friend I've ever had."

She looked at me with her pretty, sparkly

eyes and said, "Munchkin, I'm even better than a best friend—I'm your guardian angel."

At first I was a little worried that Daddy had brought her home just to guard over me. For some reason that made her laugh. She explained that God sends guardian angels to remind people of God's love for them. The angels love, help and watch over people. That was a good description, because Faith is always there for me, and I know she loves me a whole bunch, even if she won't show herself to the rest of my family.

Faith is awesome at helping me figure stuff out when I don't know what to do. The only thing

that gets a little frustrating is when I think Faith has the right answers about what I'm supposed to do—but she won't tell me. Instead, she says her job is just to give me a little nudge in the right direction. I'm supposed to pray for guidance and then learn to make my own decisions. It seems to me that if God sent Faith to help me, she may as well just tell me what to do! It would be a whole lot easier, and I know I'd get into a lot less trouble, that's for sure.

If Anna really had squished her, I didn't know what I'd do! I tried to catch my breath as a big, yucky lump got stuck in my throat and more tears started leaking out of my eyes.

"Pssst!"

I felt a tap on my shoulder, and I turned around to scowl at Anna. But it wasn't Anna who had tapped my shoulder!

"Faith! She didn't squish you!"

I wiped my eyes and reached out to give her a giant hug!

CHAPTER TWO
A Little Bit of Faith

Faith's wings weren't even crumpled. I was so glad that Anna hadn't squished her.

"Of course she didn't squish me," Faith giggled. "Didn't you know? It's not my day to be a pancake."

"Ruff! Ruff!" Patches added with his tail wagging back and forth. He likes Faith almost as much as I do.

"What would I ever do without you?" I said.

"Aren't you glad you don't have to? You're stuck with me—just like glue!" Faith said with a big squeeze, and then she kissed the top of my head.

"Uh-oh," Faith said. "Now, where did that sweet little smile of yours go, Munchkin? Do I have bad breath?"

"Did you brush your teeth?"

"I most certainly did," Faith smiled.

"Then it's not bad breath!"

"Then what gives? How come you're not smiling anymore?"

"School," I pouted and looked away. Faith's eyes followed mine to where my books were sitting, still open from the night before. "They don't do math the same way I did it at my old school, Faith."

"Lucky you!"

"How do you figure?"

"You get to learn two different ways to do it. How can you go wrong?" Faith said.

"I'd rather do without that, thank you. I'd rather do without math altogether! I'd rather do without living in this whole crummy town!"

"Come on, Katie, think about what you're saying."

"Think about what? How much I hate that new school? Or the fact that none of the other girls will talk to me? I don't have any friends there!"

"But you will. You said you liked your teacher. And think about how much you enjoy spending time with your Aunt Ella. And I know you're happy about your Daddy's new job at Camp SonShine over on Lake Lightning."

"Yeah, but . . ."

"But nothing. Before you know it, you'll love it here, too. You just need a little bit of faith. Everyone will find out how sweet and thoughtful and fun you are to be around."

"I wish we could always be together, Faith. Why can't you just come to school with me? Please?"

"No, Katie. You have to go on your own. We have a deal. I'm *your* guardian angel, so you're the only one who can see me. Besides, if I went to school with you, people would think you were walking around talking to yourself. Then how will you make new friends?"

"It probably wouldn't be much different," I pouted.

"Miss Katie Marie Bennett! All you need is *faith*. Hang onto faith in yourself and faith that God has a very special plan for you. You're a beautiful little girl, inside and out. You will make lots of good friends."

"Katie! It's time for school," Anna yelled. "I don't want to be late."

Faith flew over and gave me another kiss right on the tippy-top of my head. She had a big smile on her face and said, "I believe in you, Katie. Don't ever forget that."

"I won't," I said. I knew that Faith and God believed in me. I just wasn't so sure that I believed in me. As I rushed downstairs to meet Anna, I thought, *Have a little faith. Then maybe, just maybe, everything will work out.*

CHAPTER THREE
A Special Surprise

It was another crummy day at school. When we worked on math, I felt like I was lost in a forest of numbers. My old school made it much easier. I kept trying to leave myself clues to help me find my way, like Hansel and Gretel. But the mean math witch inside my head just waved her broom and swept them all away. When I went to the chalkboard to show Miss Marla my work, I could hear some snickers behind me.

Miss Marla scolded the snickerers and told me that it would take time to learn the way they did things. At recess, she brought me over to a bunch of girls who were playing jump rope. When it was my turn, I messed up right away, so they made me a twirler the rest of the time.

In the afternoon when the kids picked teams

during gym class, I was the last to get picked. During art, one of the girls needed red paint. I rushed to share mine and wound up spilling it all over the floor.

It was Friday and I couldn't wait to go home for the weekend. As I walked up the front sidewalk, Aunt Ella was waiting for me. She waved and I ran right into her arms. She smelled of soap and a touch of cinnamon. It made me smile.

"You look lovely!" she said, laughing, as she twirled me around. "What a sight to behold!"

"Where's Mom?"

"She's picking up a package and will be home any minute. C'mon over to the table and join Faith and me. She invited me to a little tea party."

Aunt Ella was the only person who believed that Faith was real. My Mom and Daddy *said* they believed me, but I could tell they were just playing along.

Mom got real frustrated when I ordered food for Faith at restaurants. Daddy got upset when I begged him to install a seatbelt for Faith in our van. Everybody got mad when I asked if Faith could have her own room in our new house.

"Mmmm! These smell delicious!" I said after taking a big whiff of Aunt Ella's homemade treats.

"You're a darlin'! Thank you," Aunt Ella beamed. "I baked these strawberry muffins just for you, but Faith won't eat hers."

"I'm allergic!" Faith said with a tiny sneeze.

"She's allergic to strawberries," I explained. I reached over and put Faith's muffin on my plate. They were still warm and the strawberry goo dribbled down my wrist when I took a bite. Yummy!

"I'm home!" Mom called to us from inside the house. When she appeared at the door, she had a tiny little package with a big bow. "Hi, honey! Wow, Ella, these look scrumptious!"

"They are, Mom! What's in the package?"

She sat down at the table, took a taste of her muffin, a sip of tea, and said, "Your aunt and I have been creating a special surprise for you."

"It will remind you that God made you very precious to us," Aunt Ella added with a wink.

Mom handed me the package, and I heard a tiny jingle. It sounded a little like bells—jingle bells!

"Go ahead, open it up!"

I took off the green and white bow, then I ripped through the paper. Imagine—a present in the middle of the year! That had never happened before. I opened the lid and saw a pretty, sparkling bracelet with amazing little charms—each one shaped in a different way with a word engraved on the back.

"Wow! Thank you so much! It's so pretty. I love it!"

"Each charm describes something special about you, Katie," Aunt Ella said.

I looked closer to see. "This charm is shaped like a flower and on the back it says I'm caring. This one is a heart and says I love others, and here's a hand that says I'm a good helper. Ooo! Here's a charm that says I have a good imagination! Wait!

There's one more. It's a smiling sun that says I'm
funny! Thank you, Mom! Thank you, Aunt Ella!"

I gave them a great big hug. It was a very
special gift.

"Let me help you to put it on, Katie," Mom
said. She gently placed the bracelet around my
wrist. The dainty charms dangled down and made
a tinkling sound when I moved.

I giggled. One of the worst days of my life had turned out to be extra great! "Wow! It feels like it's my birthday! The bracelet is so arrogant!"

"You mean *el*egant, sweetie, and now you'll remember just how precious you are every time you see those charms or hear them clinking together," Aunt Ella said.

They continued to "Ooo!" and "Ahh!" as I dangled it in the air. Even Faith said it was the prettiest bracelet she'd ever seen. Mom explained that Aunt Ella had made it at her craft shop—a little store she owned in downtown Shine. Aunt Ella makes and sells some of the coolest stuff there. Everyone goes to *Ella's Craft Creations* whenever they are looking for a special gift or need supplies to make something.

"The people who love and care about you can add charms to your bracelet anytime they discover another new, wonderful quality about you," Aunt Ella explained.

It was the most perfect gift I'd ever received. I stood up and walked over to Faith so she could have a better look. "Isn't it beautiful, Faith?" I asked, holding up my wrist.

"I didn't even notice Faith was here," Mom said, winking at Aunt Ella. I'm not sure why she winked, but grown-ups seem to do that a lot.

"She's been here the whole time," I giggled.

Mom looked at the chair and then under the table. "Hmm, I still don't see her, but that's okay. I know your angel is real to you, honey, and I'm sure she loves you very much. But right now I want you to concentrate on making *new* friends at school. You can show them your bracelet and Aunt Ella can come up with a brand new charm for friendship."

"Oh, yes! That would be a nice one!" Aunt Ella said, clasping her hands together. "In fact, I have a splendid idea for how you might make some new friends. What do you think about the idea of starting your very own club?"

"A club? I don't know... At my old school that would have been fun," I said. "But here . . . well, the kids are . . . different. They won't come to any club of mine, Aunt Ella."

"It's an excellent idea!" Mom chimed in. "Katie, this could be a lot of fun. Plus, this is a great way to make new friends."

"What kind of club? What would we do?"

"You could celebrate how special God made each of you!" Mom said.

"And each member could wear a charm bracelet to show how *she* is created unique and precious," Aunt Ella added. "Then you could use your precious gifts to help others."

"Clubs are a lot of fun!" Mom said. "You can do so many things together and add charms to your bracelets as each one discovers a new special gift."

"Why not call it the Precious Girls Club?" Aunt Ella announced—a lot more excited than *I* felt about it.

"Yeah, but I still don't know how to start a club if the kids at school won't even talk to me."

"It will take a little work but you can start small and build as you go. We'll help you, honey. Your dad and I are used to working with kids at the camp, so we can help you to plan some fun activities . . ."

"And I'll bake some of your favorite treats," Aunt Ella offered.

Mom gave me a big squeeze from behind. "We can decorate the house, and Anna will help, too. Every girl is precious, Katie. And there is nothing better than using your precious gifts to help others."

I did like the idea. I just wasn't convinced it would work.

CHAPTER FOUR
Afraid of Failing

When I got upstairs, I held out my hand to admire my bracelet. No one had ever given me something so special like this before—and it wasn't even my birthday! It made me feel a little grown up.

I looked at each charm and sighed, "The kids at school sure don't think I'm precious."

I felt a little breeze and then saw Faith zoom by, spin and do a triple flying loop as she yelled, "Wahoo!" and landed on my bed.

"What's all that about?" I asked.

"Aren't you thrilled about the new Precious Girls Club?" Faith laughed, out of breath. "What's wrong, sweetie?"

I looked at Faith's big, blue eyes. She was so willing to help, and I don't think I ever felt like I needed her more than right now.

"I'm really confused, Faith."

"About what?"

"Everything! I don't know why the girls don't like me, and I'm tired of trying so hard—it makes my heart hurt."

Faith rested her head against me. "The kids don't *dis*like you—they just don't *know* you."

"I like the idea of a club. But what if no one will come? Then I'll feel worse than I do now."

"We'll make it so much fun that they can't resist!"

"Really?"

Faith jumped up and soared through the air, zipping from one end of the room to the other. She whooshed by with a quick turn, a twirl and another spin around the room. She did that a lot when she was super happy.

"Do you remember what I said about needing a little bit of faith?"

"Yes."

"It's time to put that faith to the test, Munchkin. You've got to believe in yourself and God—because with God's help you can do anything you put your heart and mind to."

"Okay, Faith. I will!" I walked over to my dresser and carefully took off my new charm bracelet. I set it right on top of my rainbow jewelry box so that it wouldn't get dirty while I helped Mom with dinner. Then I would start work on the club activities.

"See that rainbow?" Faith asked.

"Sure."

"Do you know that the rainbow is a promise from God?"

I thought back to the stories I'd learned from Mom and Daddy or had heard at church. The rainbow was in the story about Noah and the ark. "Yes! I remember. God sent a rainbow as a promise that He would never flood the earth again."

"Right! And God always keeps His promises,

Katie. He created you, and He loves you. God has a special plan for you. But you need a little bit of faith and have to trust Him."

I smiled at her. She was right. "I know, and I promise to do my best." We hugged and got right to work. There were invitations, posters and announcements to be made. Then we had to plan for the first meeting!

My entire family got involved in making things for the first Precious Girls Club activities. Even Anna chipped in. When the weekend was over, Anna carried things to school and promised to help me put the posters up. We hung them everywhere. As I tacked the last one up in my classroom, I heard some of the kids talking.

"What's the new kid doing?" Jenny McBride asked her friends. "What's the Precious Girls Club?"

"Beats me," Kirina answered. "Let's see if anyone else knows anything about it or is talking about joining."

Miss Marla came in the room. Jenny leaped forward and volunteered to pass out papers— of course.

"Why, thank you, Jenny. I appreciate your help," Miss Marla said.

I didn't know Jenny McBride very well, but one thing seemed obvious. Just because her daddy owned a bunch of the businesses in downtown Shine, she seemed to feel that she could do whatever she wanted. She could be really mean and bossy to the other kids, but when a teacher or some other grownup came around, she'd become sweet as pie.

We took our seats, and Miss Marla announced, "It looks like a new club is forming—the Precious Girls Club. It's being hosted by Katie Bennett. It sounds wonderful, Katie! I hope you girls will support Katie by joining her Friday afternoon at the first meeting."

The first meeting was just four days away. I looked around the room at the other girls and wondered if any of them would be there.

CHAPTER FIVE
Wanting to Believe

I woke up Friday morning feeling like my old rag doll that sat in the bottom of my closet under a heap of forgotten clothes. I didn't sleep much, and when I did, I had terrible nightmares about what a disaster the day was going to be. I got out of bed, felt a little dizzy and sat back down again.

Faith snuck up from behind me and whispered, "You still believe in yourself, don't you?"

I squeezed my eyes shut tight. Just a little bit of faith . . . I wanted to believe. I really wanted to believe . . .

"What are you doing?" Anna asked, poking her head into my room. (I just opened my eyes and scowled at her.) "Mom made pancakes for breakfast. She said to hurry up so you can eat them warm."

"Okay, Anna," I said. "I'll be right down."

Faith took my hand in hers and said, "Just use that sparkling personality and you'll make some friends." She opened my fingers and placed my new charm bracelet in my palm. "And don't forget to wear this!"

"I want to believe, Faith. I really do."

"Then you're off to a good start!"

The clock ticked by s-o-o-o-o slowly as I waited for the end of Friday bell to ring. Would someone ask me for directions to my house or ask to walk home with me? Lunchtime and recess came and went. No one said a word to me.

When the bell finally rang, it made me jump! I tried to remember what everyone had said, especially Faith. I wanted to believe. If only I could convince myself.

I headed for home and peeked to see if anyone was following me. Nope. I picked up my pace, not wanting the girls to beat me to the house. If they had a ride, they would get there first.

I rushed up the sidewalk. The signs were hung. The balloons were out. I burst through the door, out of breath. The house looked so nice! The big sign we made was strung across the doorway, and Aunt Ella's baking filled the house with the most delicious smells.

"Hi, honey!" Mom said. "You got home fast."

"I wanted to be here when the girls arrived," I said, huffing and puffing. I hugged Mom and Aunt Ella. Everything was ready, just as planned.

Faith gave me a wink as she flew through the air and straightened several of the streamers strung from corner to corner.

Fifteen minutes passed.

Then thirty.

Aunt Ella couldn't keep from peeking out the window.

Another half hour passed. It was obvious no one was coming.

"Oh, honey, I'm so sorry," Mom said. "Maybe we didn't give the girls enough notice for the first meeting."

I couldn't stop the tears from squirting out of my eyes, no matter how hard I tried. I got lots of hugs from Mom, Aunt Ella and Faith. But it didn't help. There was nothing they could say to make it stop hurting. I scooped up Patches and went to my room.

Patches always licked my face when I cried. I think it was his way of making me feel better. Or maybe he just liked the taste of my teardrops.

I felt a familiar tap on my shoulder and knew that Faith was there with me. I turned around to see her pretty face. "I tried to have faith, Faith. I really did."

"Clubs take time to catch on," Faith said.

"Catch on?" I started to yell. "How can it catch on when no one will talk to me?"

"We'll figure it out," she said. "What did you do to help the girls get to know you and show them that you believed in yourself?"

"Huh?"

"Did you *invite* any of the girls to come to your meeting?"

"No! They don't talk to me. Aren't you listening?"

"I'm listening, Munchkin. I just don't think you want to hear what I'm saying."

I pulled away from her and pulled Patches closer, snuggling close to him. No one understood what it was like to be the new kid at school.

"You need to help the other kids notice how special you are. I know it's not easy, but I know you can do it."

"Faith, I've been trying!"

"Then we have to think of something new . . . something different . . . something so special and precious about you that the other kids just can't help but notice!"

"You're right! Faith, that's it! I can tell them about YOU! That will get their attention. If you come to my first meeting, I know all the kids will want to meet you. Please, Faith!"

It didn't matter how much I begged, Faith said no. She wouldn't budge on her answer. In fact, she made me promise not to say a peep about her to any of the girls.

"I promise," I said.

"I'm not the one looking for new friends, Munchkin," Faith said, taking a tissue to dry my tears. Her beautiful blond hair glistened in the sunlight passing through my window. She never got angry with me. She never lost her patience. She always knew what to say. "Even if your friends *could* see me (which they *can't*), you don't want them to be a part of the club because of me—you want them to join out of friendship with you—and each other."

"I suppose," I sniffed.

"If you put those special gifts to work, you'll get the girls to notice what a good friend you can be."

I looked at each little charm—a flower that said I'm caring, a heart that said I love others, a hand that said I'm a good helper, a charm with a paint brush that said I have a good imagination, and a sunshine that said I'm funny. How could my special gifts help me make new friends?

Faith read my thoughts. "You've got to use those gifts during the week to help the girls get to know you. Don't just sit around waiting for them to come to you. Be kind and helpful, Katie. Show them that you're caring, thoughtful and fun. *Be precious*, Katie. That's the best way to make new friends."

I guess she was right. I wasn't really doing anything to make friends or help the other girls get to know me. "Okay, Faith," I said. "I'll try."

Later that evening a light rain passed through town, leaving a beautiful rainbow behind. The pastel colors filled the sky from one side to the other. When I saw the rainbow, I knew it was a reminder from God that He kept His promises.

That night I said a prayer. I thanked God for His promises and then I promised Him that I would try harder to show the other girls who I was by being precious in the ways God made me.

When I woke up, I called, "Faith! Where are you?" I gently shook the beautiful snow globe where a tiny version of my special angel flew about in the snow. The globe twinkled to life. There was a big WHOOOOSH and Faith was right beside me.

"What's the emergency?" she asked, yawning.

"I have a super idea. Let's decorate the new invitations and posters for the next club meeting with rainbows! If the Precious Girls Club is all about the gifts God gave us to be precious—then we should celebrate God's promise that He has a special plan for us. Last night I saw the most beautiful rainbow in the sky! I remembered that the rainbow is a sign of God's promises—but it's also a sign that we have to have a little bit of faith to make things happen!"

"That's my girl!" Faith said as she wrapped her arms around my neck. "Keep thinking like that, and this week is going to be much better than last week."

Once again, my entire family got involved in helping me get ready for the meeting. They really liked my idea about using rainbows to show that we need to have faith in God's promises if we're going to be the best we can be with the gifts He gave us.

We made pretty rainbow invitations and posters. I helped Aunt Ella make friendship bracelets to give the girls. This would give me a chance to invite them to the club and remind them to come on Friday. Anna stitched a rainbow on my backpack, and Daddy painted a big rainbow sign to hang at school.

For the first time since we had moved, I was excited about going to school on Monday morning!

CHAPTER SIX
Rainbows and Promises

After I finished putting up the new posters on Monday morning, I spotted Kirina and Becca jumping rope. They had the rope tied to a post, because they didn't have anyone else to help twirl it.

I took a deep breath and walked over. When Becca stepped on the rope, they stopped and noticed me watching.

"Umm . . . hi!" I said. "I'm having another club meeting this Friday after school. I hope you can come. Here's a friendship bracelet that I made to help you remember," I added, giving each of them one.

"This is nice!" Kirina said, slipping it onto her wrist.

"Thanks, Katie," Becca said, putting hers on, too.

"Do you need help twirling? I can help."

"Sure! That sounds great!" Kirina said, switching places with Becca.

I took the other end and started to twirl. Kirina was a good jumper, but when she missed, she came right over and took my place so I could take a turn. This time, I jumped pretty well. We played until the first bell rang, then ran inside.

When recess came, Becca invited me to play again! As we played, I found out that Becca and Kirina had grown up right next to each other. They said they'd been friends ever since they'd started dance classes when they were little. Kirina told me she played soccer and did gymnastics, too. I couldn't believe how busy she was every week!

When the end-of-school bell rang on Tuesday, Bailey spilled her folder and loose papers went everywhere. I rushed over to help. "I use a notebook with a center binder to keep my papers in," I said. "Do you need one? I think I have an extra."

"Really?" Bailey asked. She looked surprised.

I checked my backpack. Sure enough, Mom always had an extra everything in my backpack

"just in case." I figured this was a good "just in case" time. I gave Bailey a friendship bracelet and invited her to the club meeting Friday.

"Wow! This is cool. Did you make it?" Bailey asked.

"Yep! My aunt helped me."

"It fits good—thanks!"

That was the most I'd heard Bailey say since school had started. She was a real shy girl and didn't seem to have many friends. She almost always looked as lonely as I felt. We walked partway home together and she told me about her big family. I couldn't imagine what it was like to have six brothers and sisters! When she turned to head toward her house, she thanked me for the bracelet.

"I never feel like I fit in anywhere outside my family," Bailey confided.

"Then, come to the club on Friday! We'll have fun—and I guarantee it will be a great place to feel like you belong."

On Wednesday morning I heard Jenny ask some girls where they had gotten their bracelets. She glared at me from across the room. I reached into my pocket to get one for her, but Miss Marla said it was time for our spelling lesson.

During lunchtime, Jenny was sitting with a bunch of other girls. I headed over to sit with them, but Jenny said there wasn't enough room for me. I didn't want to make her mad, so I took my tray and found another table.

As I was taking my sandwich out, I saw that Lidia didn't have a lunch. I scooted down the bench to sit across from her.

"Aren't you hungry?" I asked.

"I forgot my lunch money," she answered.

I wasn't sure if she was telling the truth or not. The clothes she wore were always old and a little tattered. I heard a couple of kids teasing her one day about not having any money. They were being super mean.

"I'll share my lunch with you," I offered. "My Mom always packs more than I can eat anyway."

"Really?" she asked. "That's really nice of you."

I gave her half of my sandwich, some apple slices, a cookie and a friendship bracelet. Then I told her about the club and invited her on Friday.

"Wow! Thanks," she said. "It looks pretty! Thank you."

The bracelet did look nice on her. She never wore jewelry or girlish things. Her hair was cut real short and she usually wore suspenders and sneakers to school. She really liked the bracelet and told me she didn't get anything new very often.

"That's because I live with my Grandma and Grandpa, and they don't have much money. They're real nice, though. They took me and my brothers and sisters to live with them when we were little. My parents were in a bad accident."

"Gee, Lidia. I'm real sorry to hear that."

"Thanks, Katie. I don't remember them. We're lucky that my Grandma and Grandpa have always been there for us. They've been just like parents."

When lunch was over, Lidia thanked me again for the lunch, the bracelet and the invitation. She even said she would try to come!

"That's great! I hope you can!"

After school, Jenny sat on a bench waiting for her ride home. I got up my courage and walked over to invite her to the meeting.

"Hi, Jenny! I've been wanting to give you this bracelet all week." I handed her the bracelet and felt my stomach do a flip-flop.

Jenny held it up between her dainty fingers and scrunched up her face. "I don't know," she said. "I have much prettier things to wear than this."

"Oh, I know. You dress really nice."

"Yes, I do, and this doesn't go with anything."

"Oh . . . well . . . I was afraid you felt left out. I'm giving bracelets to all the girls to help them remember to come to my club meeting on Friday."

"I never feel left out," Jenny said. "And I know all about your little club, but I have a busy schedule and so many important things to do. I'm sure you understand."

"Sure. Well, if you change your mind . . ."

"I doubt I will. Besides, I usually have

sleepovers at my house on Fridays. Most of the girls in our class come to that."

I couldn't believe what she was saying. If Jenny invited most of the girls to her house, then who would show up for the Precious Girls Club? It was useless to keep trying!

"Oh, did I hurt your feelings?" Jenny smirked. "I didn't mean to. I thought you would understand."

"I understand, all right!" I blurted out, fighting back tears. "Faith was wrong about everything. It doesn't matter how hard I try."

I quickly turned to leave, but she called me back.

"Katie! Wait a minute. Don't go yet!" she called with a softer voice.

I turned around, trying to hold the tears inside.

"Who is Faith?" Jenny asked.

"She's my *real* guardian angel. I bet *you*

don't have one of those!" Whoops! The words tumbled out of my mouth so fast that I didn't have time to think about what I was saying.

Jenny laughed at me. "Ooooohhhhhh. And will you introduce me to her if I come to your meeting?"

I was frozen in place and didn't know what to say or do. Thankfully, Jenny's ride arrived and she got up to go.

"Can't wait to meet your . . . guardian angel is it?" she asked, grinning.

"Yeah, that's right," I said, frowning back at her. Then she got in the car and disappeared.

Faith was *not* going to be pleased about this.

CHAPTER SEVEN
Trouble Ahead

"How did it go today?" Faith asked as I sat on my bed doing homework.

"Not now, Faith. I'm trying to study," I grumbled.

I felt a slight breeze behind me to the right, then the left, then the right again.

"Just tell me how it went, and then I won't bug you anymore," Faith pleaded.

I let out a sigh and turned to face her. "I made a new friend at lunch today. Her name is Lidia. She forgot her lunch money, so I shared my lunch with her."

"I'm proud of you, Munchkin!" she said and flew over to kiss the top of my head.

At that same moment, Anna burst through the door. "Katie Bennett! Why did you tell Jenny

that you have a guardian angel that she can meet on Friday?"

I glanced up at Faith who looked at me sternly. I didn't know what to say to either of them.

"It just sorta slipped out," I said weakly. "Jenny was being so mean to me. She was making plans to have all the girls over to her house Friday for a sleepover."

"So you told her you have a *real* guardian angel? Do you know how embarrassed I was when her sister called and told me that on the phone?"

"I really wasn't thinking about *you*, Anna."

"Well, what are you going to do if all the girls show up and want to meet your angel?" Anna asked. "It will serve you right, you know. Maybe you'll finally learn your lesson when the girls find out that you still go around playing make-believe like a baby."

"I'm *not* a baby, Anna!" I shouted, but she was gone.

I turned back to face Faith who was looking very disappointed with me. I felt terrible. "Faith, I'm sorry. I didn't mean to say it. But Jenny was going to ruin everything!"

"I understand that part, Munchkin."

"Really? Will you talk to her at the meeting?"

"No, sweetie, I can't. There will always be bullies or kids who stand in your way of doing what's right. That doesn't mean that you should act like them. You can't do whatever you want in order to get something. When you do, it makes you just as guilty as them."

"But I've been having faith and keeping my promise to God all week!"

"But you broke your promise to me," Faith said quietly.

"But I didn't know what else to do . . ."

"And now you've got an even bigger problem."

CHAPTER EIGHT
Countdown

When the first bell rang on Thursday morning, I saw a little boy sitting in the hall, crying.

"What's the matter?" I asked him.

He looked up and sniffed. "I can't tie my shoes and the other kids keep laughing at me."

"Don't pay attention to them. Besides, I think I can help. I had trouble tying my shoes when I was little, too. I learned a good way that helped me to remember. It's called bunny ears."

I quickly showed him how Anna had taught me when I was little. "Doesn't that make it easier?" I asked as we practiced together.

He smiled and stood up to give me a big hug. I ran down the hall to my classroom and heard him shouting, "I can tie my shoes!"

It did feel good to do what's right and help others. If only I'd stuck to doing what was right yesterday. Heading into class, I realized that Friday was just one day away. The countdown had begun. I wondered how much Jenny had told the other girls. How many would believe her? Would anyone show up at my house Friday? The questions swirled around in my head like a tornado blowing in.

• • •

At lunchtime, a tall girl came over to me at the swings. I slowed down. I recognized her from one of the older grades.

"Hi! My name is Nicola," she said.

"I'm Katie," I answered, giving up my swing to the next girl in line.

"My little brother, Bobby, said you helped him this morning. I just wanted to thank you."

"It was no problem," I said.

"Well, it was nice of you," she added. "By the way, my friends and I noticed your posters around school. Is it okay for us to join your club even though we're older?"

"Sure! All girls are invited. I'd love it if you could come."

"Great! I'll let them know," she said. "And thanks again."

• • •

During art class, we had to paint our own masterpiece. I loved art and couldn't wait to start, but the girl beside me just stared at her paper.

"What's wrong, Avery?"

"I'm not creative," she answered. "I don't like painting at all, and I can't think of anything to paint."

"Whenever I get ready to paint, I close my eyes and try to see something inside my head first. It makes it easier if you imagine it first, and then try to re-create it."

Avery decided to try it. She closed her eyes, and I asked her what she saw.

"I see the back of my eyelids," she giggled.

I laughed, too. Then I told her to think about something she thought was pretty.

"I've got it!" she answered, and started to paint. "I thought about the pretty rainbows on the posters you put up around school."

Avery created a beautiful picture of a rainbow as she asked me questions about the Precious Girls Club. When she was done, she said her picture was the best one she'd ever made.

"You have such a good imagination, Katie. I wish I could be like that."

"My Aunt Ella says that imagination is just like a muscle. The more you exercise it, the stronger it gets."

"You must exercise yours a lot!"

"Maybe we can exercise together sometime," I laughed.

"Okay!"

"And you can help me learn how to do my math problems," I said. "You sure are good at that!"

Avery blushed, but agreed to help me anytime I needed it.

• • •

After school, I was in a hurry to get home.
There was a lot to do to get ready. I rushed
through the school hall, turned the corner and . . .

CRASH!—walked right into Jenny McBride. Her books went flying and we both fell to the floor.

"Look what you did!" she shrieked. "Why don't you watch where you're going?"

"I'm really sorry, Jenny," I said, standing up.

I offered to give Jenny a hand, but she pushed it away. As she straightened her skirt and hair, I scrambled to pick up her books and papers.

"Don't *miss* anything!" she sniffed.

Some of the other girls gathered around to see what had happened.

"She's not your slave, Jenny," Kirina said.

"No," Jenny laughed. "She's just a clumsy kid with a dumb club and a make-believe angel!"

"No, she's not," Becca protested. "She's nice and her club sounds fun."

Jenny pointed to a paper. "Over there—you missed one."

I walked over to get it as Jenny told the kids about her Friday sleepover.

"I think I'd rather give Katie's club a try this week," Lidia said.

A couple other girls said, "Me, too!" as I stood up to hand Jenny her last paper. She ripped it from my hand and glared at me, just as Nicola walked up with some of her friends.

"Jenny McBride, are you causing trouble again?" she asked.

Jenny may have acted like a queen bee in my class, but she was definitely a little nervous around the older girls.

"It's okay, Nicola. It was my fault," I said. "I'm sorry I ran into you, Jenny."

Jenny didn't know what to say, so she just put her books and papers back in order as the girls started walking away.

When we were alone again, she asked, "Why did you do that?"

"Do what?"

"Why were you nice to me?"

I shrugged my shoulders. "I know what it's like to feel that nothing is going your way."

"Oh . . . right. Well, I'm . . . ah . . . sorry too, I guess. It's just that I usually have a sleepover on Fridays."

I held her backpack as she put her books and folders inside.

"Yeah. You told me about that. Okay, then, see ya!" I turned to go.

"Hey, wait a minute! If I come to your house tomorrow, will I really get to meet your guardian angel?"

"Ummm . . . I don't know. She's sorta shy." I didn't know what to say. "Why don't you come by and see what happens?"

And, guess what! Jenny McBride agreed to come to my house for the first meeting of the Precious Girls Club. It was either going to be a huge success—or the disaster of my life!

CHAPTER NINE
The Precious Girls Club

Friday.

The big day!

I was more nervous than on the first day of school.

"Everything will be okay," Faith assured me.

"Well, all week I've tried to remember the ways that God made me precious. I used those things to reach out to the other girls at school, and I think it worked. I showed them how much fun it is to be precious. I just hope they have fun when they get here."

"Don't stop believing now, Munchkin!" Faith said.

"I won't."

After school, ten girls came to the house. Mom was ready to greet them. Rainbows were hanging everywhere and Aunt Ella had made a big plate of rainbow cookies.

Mom explained to the girls that God had made each one of them to be precious in different ways by giving them special gifts and talents they could use every day.

Aunt Ella said she would help each girl come up with a list of her own special qualities. Then she'd help us make charm bracelets to wear as reminders that God made all of us precious.

"And to start things off, I'm giving each of you a charm for your bracelet," Aunt Ella said. "This is a rainbow charm to remind you of God's love and promises."

The girls were super excited to get their bracelets, and I was eager to add my new charm.

Then we played games, shared funny stories and ate Aunt Ella's delicious cookies.

"Enjoy your cookies, girls!" Aunt Ella said.

"And while you're talking, try to think of a project you would like to do next week to help others," Mom said as she and Aunt Ella went into the kitchen.

The girls started calling out different ideas. Suddenly, Jenny McBride said, "When do we get to meet your guardian angel?"

All eyes looked at me.

I looked at Faith. She was sitting on the piano bench, watching. She just shrugged her shoulders. I would have to figure this out on my own!

"Well?" Jenny asked.

That's when we heard a pretty little tune that grew louder as Anna entered the room, holding my musical snow globe with Faith dancing about inside.

"Oooo! She's beautiful, Katie!" Becca said, jumping up to get a closer look. Becca's brown eyes opened wide as she looked at the angel and put her hand on my shoulder.

The other girls followed, and everyone gathered around to see the best present that Daddy had ever given me.

"*That's* your guardian angel?" Jenny asked.

"Of course. I have one, too," Anna said. "Her name is Hope. Would you like to see her?"

"Sure!" the girls chorused.

Anna handed the snow globe to Jenny, who watched my little angel dance around the glittering

snowflakes, as Anna ran up to get her own angel. A few moments later, she returned to show the girls Hope.

"Wow! She's pretty, too!" Lidia said.

As the girls admired the angels, I snuck over to give Anna a little squeeze and whisper a big "Thank you" in her ear. Faith flew over and whispered, "Good job today!" and kissed the very tippy-top of my head.

Our club decided to work on a puppet project at the next meeting. Kirina wanted to

present a show for the little kids who were sick at the hospital.

The first meeting was a success! Even better, I finally made some new friends and couldn't wait to get to know them better. I also learned how good it felt to be precious and reach out to others.

• • •

The next day, some of the girls invited me to the roller skating rink. While we were there, Mr. Boxer, the president of the Shine Hospital, came by to talk to the manager. What a great chance to tell him about our puppet show idea for the kids at the hospital!

Kirina and I ran over to tell him—and to ask when we could put on the show. We weren't ready for his answer.

"We don't have time for that," he mumbled. "I'm sorry—I am a very busy man."

"But, Mr. Boxer, we'll plan the whole thing," I said as Kirina nodded. "We can perform the show during visiting hours in the big room—you know, where the kids watch television."

I felt a little sorry for Mr. Boxer. He looked so worried and flustered.

"No. Oh, no, no, no," he said, waving his hand. "Try the school. They might let you put on a play."

"It's not a play—" I started, but Kirina nudged me away.

"I think we have more than one project to work on," she whispered. "The puppet show—and Mr. Boxer."

Kirina and I hurried back to the other girls. We told them what had happened and everyone agreed it was going to be a big challenge to convince Mr. Boxer that we could do a puppet show for the kids. Faith whispered to me later that we would just have to be *extra* precious when it came to convincing *him*. But that's a story for another day.

That night, my family gathered around at bedtime to say, "I love you," and pray. We all got big hugs and kisses. Then Mom and Daddy started out with the same prayer we said every night:

More precious than silver,
more precious than gold—
God made you special
and precious to hold.
You were created a bright shining star—
My little angel, be just who you are!
Embrace each new day
and give it your best,
Open your heart
and let God do the rest.
I'll cherish you always.
I'll be by your side.
I'll love you forever,
my daughter, my pride.